La  Terre Trem— blante

Translated from French

Unsteady Earth
Marie-Jeanne Urech

Translated from French by
Andrea Reece

First published in English by Strangers Press, Norwich, 2022
part of UEA Publishing Project

First published in Switzerland by Hélice Hélas
as *La Terre Tremblante* in 2018

All rights reserved
Author © Marie-Jeanne Urech, 2018
Translator © Andrea Reece, 2022

Printed by
Swallowtail, Norwich

Series editors
Nathan Hamilton & Lucy Rand

Editorial assistance
Lily Alden, Erin Maniatopoulou and Emma Seager

Proofread by
Senica Maltese

Cover design and typesetting
Glen Robinson (aka GRRR.UK)

Design Copyright © Glen Robinson, 2022

The rights of Marie-Jeanne Urech to be identified as the author and Andrea Reece to be identified as the translator of this work have been asserted in accordance with the Copyright, Designs and Patents Act, 1988. This booklet is sold subject to the condition that it shall not, by way of trade or otherwise, be lent, resold, hired out, stored in a retrieval system, or otherwise circulated without the publisher's prior consent in any form of binding or cover other than that in which it is published and without a similar condition including this condition being imposed on the subsequent purchaser.

ISBN: 978-1-913861-42-1

YOU LEFT OUR VILLAGE ONE EIGHTH OF MAY, *shortly after the burial. Those present would later say the coffin had dropped into the hole like an anchor. Was it the fear of seeing him re-surface one day that made you decide to leave? Instead of joining the others in the café, you were spotted heading up the mountain path, one hand still black from this soil that nourishes the dead better than the living.*

You first stopped halfway up to catch your breath. Down below, the red train ploughed its way through the valley, sowing the fields with seasonal workers whom it would return to their families once autumn came. The village seemed so small that you could have put it in your pocket, but what was the point of weighing yourself down with a dairy farm, a slaughterhouse, a café and everyone inside when you thought you'd be back that evening or the following morning at the latest, after you'd seen what lay hidden on the other side of the mountain?

For as long as you could remember, you'd stared up at the hut perched on the ridge, occasionally lit up by a passing traveller, most often waiting for one. Every morning, its windows reflected the first rays of the sun, before they swung downwards, awakening our valley at three minutes past ten. You'd dreamt of climbing up there one day to embrace the invisible horizon, to see what it was like on the other side, beyond the only mountain you'd ever known.

You unbuttoned your waistcoat and discarded your tie as uncomfortable remnants of the funeral then continued your ascent through the fir trees. When you finally reached the summit, shortly before dusk, you must have been hugely disappointed: the mountain had merely concealed yet another mountain that foreshortened your horizon in turn. You didn't yet know this, but behind every mountain lay another. Rock after rock after rock loomed before you. Why didn't you turn back to the village? You hadn't even taken anything to drink. The lantern in the hut shone all night long. In the morning, we saw you come out, stare at the valley below, and give us an expansive wave before vanishing over the other side.

So began your journey around the world, Bartholomé. You set out on a day trip, your only baggage the key to a house that your adventures would increasingly distance you from. You contradicted all the scientists who claim the Earth is round, because you never returned to your point of departure.

BEHIND THE FIRST MOUNTAIN

I emerged onto a road. A beautifully tarmacked road, quite different from the stony tracks in our valley. The traffic was heavy. Spacious saloons, stacked high with children, baggage, paddles, bikes, and dogs, advanced in an orderly fashion, engines choking in the unseasonably hot weather. Occasionally, one would stop for a moment and those behind would grind to a halt in a cacophony of horns, curses and raised fists. The queue would start crawling forward again in the shade of the cypress trees that served as milestones. The traffic was heavy, as I was saying, but in one direction only. The lane opposite was as sparsely populated as our priest's head. An old man sat on a bench beside the empty carriageway. Hands crossed over the pommel of his walking stick, he stared in the direction from which nothing came. He offered me a seat.

'Spot of luck they put these benches here,' he said, by way of greeting.

'Shouldn't they have turned them to face the view?' I ventured, indicating the countryside stretching out behind him.

'The good thing is there's room for three. It makes the wait seem shorter.'

'For the bus?'

'There is no bus.'

'Then what are you waiting for?'

'My son.' The old man turned towards me and looked me up and down. 'Have you been to a wedding?'

'A funeral.' I realised I was still in my mourning suit.

'Some people have all the luck.'

'Luck? I don't understand.'

He went back to scrutinising the horizon, but nothing came.

'The dead don't need to wait. And they get to lie down, much more comfortable when you've got back pain like mine.'

Horns sounded, a sign that the smooth progression of saloons had once again been held up by a stationary car. Why didn't they overtake, since there were no vehicles coming the other way? It was bad luck to cross the white line, the old man told me.

'What time is your son arriving?'

'When the holidays are over.'

'Today?' I asked.

'Today, tomorrow, next week, I don't know. Depends on his overtime, the number of public holidays in the year, how many days off he's already had, sick days that need deducting. It's a complicated calculation. That's all he told me.'

'Are you going to wait here for him the whole time?'

'That's a strange question. Of course. Look!' he said, pointing his stick at the traffic that was moving slowly again. 'A new one!'

Through the stream of cars, we caught a glimpse of a motionless figure, stuck on the other side of the road like a telegraph pole, a cypress tree or a milestone. She was staring at the point where all the cars vanished and none returned. The old man beckoned her over. Half an hour later, she joined us. She was old like my grandmother but not dressed in black. Her hands were shaking.

'It'll be better with two of us,' the old man said to her reassuringly, indicating a space on the bench.

'Do you know each other?' I asked.

'No need. She's like me, she's been abandoned by the roadside on the way to the holidays.'

'He's not from round here,' the old man explained to the woman, who was looking at me oddly. 'They bury them where he comes from.'

'They bought a dog,' sobbed the woman. 'He took my place.'

'Huh! That old trick! Then they take advantage of our weak bladders to dump us in the middle of nowhere and make off,' the old man explained. 'We're too much of a burden for our families. Especially when the holidays come round.'

'The children were upset, I could tell,' she sighed.

'So we wait on this side of the road, because some of them pick us up on the way back,' the old man said. 'Remorse,' he added, by way of explanation.

'And what if no one comes?'

'We end up in the village, but we don't want to be there.'

'Why? What happens?'

'They make us work, parading around with sandwich boards, night and day, in all weathers.'

※

I spent a troubled night squeezed between my two unfortunate companions. What could I do? Take them home with me? They wouldn't make it over the mountain. In the morning, to my shame, I left them. The road, as I said, was lined with cypress trees but also portable toilets, making it easier to abandon the elderly folk. Many were sitting around waiting on benches. All around them, the opulent countryside glowed golden in the sun, fields bursting with wheat ready to harvest and corpulent trees sagging under the weight of already ripened fruit. The season was much more advanced here. I thought of our farmers still scrutinising the sky for any sign of showers. By mid-afternoon, the traffic had subsided and I caught sight of the first houses on the outskirts of the holiday village.

※

The main street was lined with shopfronts promising water sports equipment, postcards, electric barbecues and year-round sunshine. Holidaymakers flip-flopped from one shop to the next, dripping sweat on the souvenirs they called presents. They then sought shade in a small central park where cows were grazing. Sheer perfection! Beautiful two-tone dairy cows, accompanied by a brass band squashed into a bandstand mimicking the sound of the cowbells worn by free-roaming cattle. Children reached over the electric fence, proffering handfuls of grass in an attempt to attract the cows' attention. All of a sudden, something shiny on one of their rumps caught the light. A round metallic object. It was scarcely credible: someone had stitched a porthole onto the cow's rump. Like the porthole on a cruise ship! The boy next to me giggled and, with a look of wonder on his face, pointed out the mutilated belly to his father. All the cows were similarly equipped: a slit about fifteen centimetres across had been made in their skin to insert a porthole. The milk in each cow's belly swished around to the rhythm of its movements as it continued grazing peacefully. Like the tide coming in at sea, the level of milk rose, rapidly reaching the upper edge of the glass. The children were in a state of unbridled excitement. A farmer and his farmhands positioned themselves under the cows' udders to milk them as the children formed a line. Each was handed a glass of fresh milk. The holidaymakers appeared to enjoy the attraction, crowding around the milking as if gathered in a bar.

'What's the porthole for?' I asked the farmer.

'Window on the product. Customers like to know where it comes from and kids find it funny. Helluva job polishing all that glass though. You'd think I was a sailor not a farmer.'

'And what do the cows think?'

'Dunno. You'd have to ask them. Next month, I'm getting a delivery of synthetic ones. More efficient, apparently. And the milk comes in mint, raspberry and liquorice flavours. The kids'll love it.'

I was parched so I ordered a glass of milk. I still had a few coins buried in my pocket. The farmer looked at them suspiciously and refused to take them.

'Do you come from a long way away?' asked a child waiting in the queue behind me with a dog that was bigger than him on a leash.

'From the other side,' I said, pointing at the mountain. 'What's this place called?'

'Aspartame. It's got another name but it's a bit complicated and I can never remember it.'

'Is that your dog?'

'They just bought him for me. He's too big, isn't he? I wanted a little one that doesn't get bigger, but my parents chose him. They got the biggest one on purpose.'

'Why on purpose?'

The kid turned red and offered me his glass of milk.

'Present!' he said. 'Come and see me, we're staying down at the lake.'

✹

I walked off, thinking about the old people. I could have stolen a car to pick them up, but I couldn't drive. Our village streets were too narrow for traffic. In the winter, you could barely put one foot in front of another in the snow-filled passages that burrowed their way through the village like cheese mites. Even tractors were of no use to us on the steep fields that we still farmed with traditional methods. How long ago did I leave? It felt like three, maybe four, days. Wasn't it time to go back, now I'd seen what was on the other side? Porthole-cows soon to be replaced by synthetic models and old people abandoned by the roadside. Yes, it was time to go back.

✹

The lake was perfectly symmetrical, hollowed out with a digger, and filled with water brought in by truck. It was dotted with boats drifting into one another like dodgems at a funfair. Transistor radios on the shore spewed out a mishmash of music and sports commentary while barbecues crackled and hissed with undercooked meats. The magnificent sunset was reflected in the huge bay windows of the lakeside holiday cabins. Once a year, a travelling entertainer called Joseph projected a film onto our church's whitewashed façade, but I think I was more fascinated by the lakeside sunset here than by Charlie Chaplin's antics on our church wall. From our village, we would watch the sun disappear behind the ridge at four in the afternoon, leaving a few anaemic pink traces in the sky before the stars were shining and darkness had fallen abruptly. Life would then transfer indoors, behind the postage-stamp windows of our economically lit houses. Here, the transition from day to night lasted an eternity. It was beautiful.

'Don't you think the sun looks like chewing gum?' I recognised the kid who had offered me his glass of milk. 'It stretches out until night comes. What's it like where you're from?'

'Like a bulb. You switch it on, it's daytime, you switch it off, it's night. There's nothing in between.'

'I love playing with switches!' he exclaimed, pulling me towards the road. 'Follow me, I've got something to show you.'

The boy led me to a hangar. In the semi-darkness, I could make out the outline of a motorboat on a trailer.

'We're going to launch it tomorrow!' the child whispered proudly.

'I can see your parents like big things!'

'It's got room for ten. You can come out with us. There's lots of space now,' he added, in a sad voice.

'Ten!' I repeated, lost in thought.

'A farmer is coming with his tractor. The trailer is too heavy for our car.' He grabbed my arm and pulled me into the road. 'Daddy doesn't like me going near the boat, it's his pride and joy!'

I held out one of my coins.

'Present!' I said. 'In case you come and visit me one day on the other side of the mountain.'

'Will you come tomorrow?'

'Tomorrow, I'll be far away.'

※

It wasn't as easy as I'd expected, but by five in the morning everything was ready. Apart from a few fishermen, too busy pulling up their nets to pay attention to me, I didn't see a soul. Aspartame woke up late, and I took advantage of the stillness to slip discreetly out of town. Dawn offered welcome light. After half an hour at a slow pace, I found myself on the long road lined with cypress trees. I quickly spotted an old man. He complimented me on my improvised vehicle, clambered on board and settled in the front, waving his stick for me to go faster. A bit farther on, two others boarded and sat in the back, wrapping scarves around their heads as a slight breeze had risen. We stopped wherever people were waiting and picked up everyone who wished to embark. Towards midday, I caught sight of the bench where the whole story had begun. My old man couldn't believe his eyes as four porthole-cows drew to a halt in front of him, towing a motorboat with fifteen happy faces peeking out. He embraced me and, as the tide was high, we raised a glass of fresh milk to toast our reunion.

The path that led back home over the mountains was just a few steps away. I could have bidden them all farewell and handed over the reins. In a day or two, I would have been heading down the path on the other side, walking through the village and telling the story of my adventures to my friends at home. But would they have believed me? The old people were back up in the boat when I hopped on board too, suddenly filled with a crazy desire to keep going.

BARTHOLOMÉ DE MÉNIBUS
30° N 140° W

We waited days for you to come back. I stood by the window, staring at the mountain through binoculars, imagining I could see you in every movement of the fir trees. They kept watch at the café too, waiting for you to walk in, expecting to hear your voice ordering your usual glass of schnapps. The widows climbed the path up to the church where they lit candles and prayed for your return. Hands shielding their eyes, the farmers surveyed the skies, fearing late rain showers. In the cemetery, the freshly turned earth was a reminder of your hasty departure; few people understood why you had left. Some saw it as a sign of desperation, but I never believed that. Every evening, when the mountain became too dark to look out for you, I stationed myself opposite your house, convinced I'd see the light come on. I waited for hours, joined on occasions by little Inès, but the tears would well up in her eyes and she soon went home. Rumours of your death soon took hold, lingering and persistent like the aroma of freshly baked bread.

On the fourteenth of May, almost a week after you had left, four men finally set out in search, having borrowed the stretcher from the doctor, who was too old to venture into the mountains. We watched them hike across the valley, hop over the stream, and follow the forest's edge to the hut, where they spent the night. One of them was Jean Tabard, your milk-brother, an experienced mountaineer, ready to do all it took to find you. The following morning, we lost sight of them as they headed over the ridge. Meanwhile, the village speculated. Crochety Christine, you know how fretful she can be, drew up a list of everyone who had gone missing in the mountains while the priest allowed himself the luxury of opening the Bible at a random verse, claiming they all contained hope. The men came back down two days later with an empty stretcher. I took this as confirmation you were still alive, others interpreted it as a conclusive sign you had died, the pain of their grieving exacerbated by the lack of a corpse.

The following day, we found the remains of a wolf dumped in the slaughterhouse. That caused a huge commotion. Despite the shepherds complaining regularly to the village president, the killing of wolves is forbidden, as you well know. Naturally everyone suspected the most vindictive among them, Rodolphe of Haut Binet, who was summoned to the village hall. In the café, people started whispering that it was old Roland – known for his hunting prowess – who'd shot the animal to make everyone suspect Rodolphe of Haut Binet. All over a land dispute, as you know! That business kept the entire village occupied, the café was packed to bursting, and they completely forgot about you, Bartholomé.

BEHIND THE THIRD MOUNTAIN

A river stopped me in my tracks. As night edged in, I searched for fallen branches to build a fire. I had barely warmed up when, before my eyes, the river lit up. Hundreds of lights were appearing here, there and everywhere on the water's surface. It made me think of the fireflies we used to see in the village. If the weather was hot enough in June, we'd go into the woods near the stream and try to spot the tiny luminous flames that looked like comets. But the lights I was seeing now weren't dancing chaotically or joyfully. They were rising into the air in orderly squares, forming luminous columns that created a huge electric structure. A forest of skyscrapers was emerging right there in front of me, occupying a tiny strip of land above the river. What a wondrous sight, this vertical town, what power, what elegance! I had heard people talk of towers like these, towers so high that you needed an oxygen mask to reach the top floors. I had imagined they looked like our mountains. Back in the valley, even the village hall, with its three concrete storeys, seemed colossal compared to our chalets built into the slope to shield them from avalanches. At daybreak, when all the twinkling fury suddenly clicked off, as if the skyscrapers had collapsed and sunk into the river, I set out.

❉

A long line of people, bedecked with bags, boxes and crates had formed by the bridge entrance. I took my place in their ranks and waited my turn, eager to explore the town. We'd barely moved in half an hour, so I asked my neighbour why.

'We have to wait for people to leave town before we can go in,' he replied, astonished that I'd asked.

'What do you mean?'

'For every person who leaves, one enters.'

'Why's that?'

'Lack of space, obviously!'

'So it could take hours,' I said, somewhat discouraged.
'Days.'

※

Fortunately, at around three in the afternoon, the town appeared to empty all of a sudden and I crossed under the entrance to the bridge. My neighbour explained that it was always easier to get in on really hot days. The locals would flock to the countryside to enjoy a spot of fresh air and wouldn't come back until evening.

'How do they get back in? They must have to wait for ages.'

'Most people who've gone in will have left by then.'

'You don't stay in the town? After all that waiting?'

'Certainly not. We only come here to buy produce at a good price.'

He stared at me, eyebrows knitted. 'What about you? What are you looking for? You don't even have a bag.'

'New experiences. I'm travelling, exploring and absorbing all the wonders. Only a few days ago, I visited a town where people run nonstop.'

'What's the point of that?'

'They're making up for lost time.'

'That's pointless.'

'I told them they were wasting their time. Instead of running in a straight line, they'd be better off going round in circles. That way they'd have an outside chance of catching up with themselves.'

'Like a dog and its tail.'

'My dream is to go to the top of one of those skyscrapers.'

'That'd be tricky. Unless you turned yourself into sausage meat.'

※

I watched him vanish into the throngs streaming around the town's main arteries, so narrow they resembled intestines. I stared wonderstruck at those improbable, abnormally large buildings with their extravagant distorting mirrors tinted in celestial hues, modern stalagmites, a bouquet of metallic flowers, an explosion of matter! Heart thumping, I too plunged into the chaos fanned by the unbearable heat. Everywhere, deliverymen pushed carts laden with goods, haggling prices with parched-voiced traders as they dashed past. Porters, hidden from view behind their packages, forced their way through the stalls before being swallowed up by the service stairs. Vegetables by the crate, meat by the carcass and rolls of charcuterie were being sold. Prices were set on the fly, fluctuating according to supply and demand, causing the crowds to surge uncontrollably. I dived in and out between bodies, animal remains and the disproportionate, intimidating, almost divine, towers that made me feel as insignificant as I felt next to any mountain. The town's streets, shrouded in their persistent shadow, reminded me of our valley: strangled, squeezed, doomed. I left because of the lack of horizon. All I had to do now was get to the top of one of these skyscrapers.

※

I spotted one with a majestic entrance, all brilliance and vanity, which must have been where the town's great and good resided. Hastily dusting down my Sunday best suit, I approached the guard, who immediately barred my entry.

'Excuse my somewhat crumpled attire, I have travelled a long distance.'

'It's not the suit that bothers me, sir. It's your face,' he replied.

'What's wrong with it?'

'You don't look like a pig to me.'

'Thank you.'

'Pigs only in here, sir.'

'Why's that?'

'It's a pig farm.'

'You keep pigs here?' I queried, not believing my ears.

'No, we don't keep them, we raise them,' a voice behind the guard said emphatically.

'Pigs move up from one floor to the next and at the top, when they're good and fat, they're butchered.' The man approached me, holding out his plastic-gloved hand. 'Martin van Beck, director of the breeding centre. With whom do I have the pleasure?'

'Bartholomé de Ménibus. I've come from over the mountains to...'

'... to be inspired by our methods! It's flattering to have a visitor from so far away. If you would care to follow me, I'll be your guide.'

'Are we going to the top?'

'Naturally, it's heart-stopping up there, quite takes the breath away!'

He wrapped me in a sheet of cellophane, propped a plastic cap on my head, held out boots, gloves and a mask that he forced me to wear. 'In case of foreign germs,' he said apologetically. 'After all, you do come from a far-off land.'

Enveloped in a triple layer of plastic that made me sweat, I entered a room that occupied the entire ground floor. It was packed with hundreds of sows frolicking on the straw and grunting. The contrast between the marble walls, the chandeliers dripping from the ceiling and the troughs oozing with muck was striking.

'This is our Testosteroom. Where we inseminate the sows.'

'It's dreadfully hot,' I said, suffocating in my mask.

'The sows need to be on heat to be fertile. Once they've been inseminated, they move up a floor to where temperatures are cooler, I can assure you.'

'I can't see any boars.'

'Testes have been replaced by test tubes here. In vitro fertilisation is the name of the game! Modernity is the thing on this side of the mountain, Monsieur de Ménibus,' he said, ushering me into a Paternoster lift that took us up to the first floor before continuing its perpetual ascent. 'Where we are now is the Gestationery. The sows stay here for their entire gestation period: three months, three weeks and three days. It takes three trimesters, almost thrice the time, to make a human baby, so although we're closely related to pigs, we're by far superior,' he chuckled. 'Do you feel cooler here?'

Sprawled on beds of straw across the whole floor, the sows occupied different spaces according to whether their bellies were one, two or three months advanced. The ones about to give birth were stationed near the lift, ready to go up to the Uddairy, where we were greeted by an infernal din.

'Twelve piglets per litter, five hundred and sixty sows,' the director said with some pride. 'I'll let you calculate the number of animals we have here. And I must add, we are a medium-sized farm. Two streets farther down is a skyscraper double the size of ours!'

Six thousand seven hundred and twenty piglets were suckling their daily litre of milk, clamped to their mothers' teats. At La Sarre Farm, Félix raised ten pigs, calling each by name and whenever he took one to the slaughterhouse, he would have the priest come to administer last rites. In a corner of the building, sows were being attached one by one to a machine that squeezed their udders.

'What's being done to them?'

'They're being milked. Once piglets have been weaned, sows still produce milk for a day. We collect it to make cheese.'

'Pig's cheese?'

'You've never heard of it? It's delicious. We'll sample some later.'

The sows, drained of their milk, headed towards the Paternoster lift to go back down to the ground floor where a sperm tube awaited them so they could continue the perpetual cycle: ground, first, second, ground. In the meantime, the newly weaned piglets sprang into the Paternoster travelling in the opposite direction to the floor above, where they began the fattening cycle. As we headed towards the top floor, we found ourselves sharing the lift with ever-fatter pigs; Martin van Beck explained that a piglet went up one floor every day. It was fattened in this way for a period of four months until it reached the one hundred and twenty-fifth and last floor, perfectly plump, top-quality pork.

'It must be a fantastic view from up there,' I said, thinking of our mountains.

'That's as may be, but what interests us more is the drop.' The floors trundled past at walking pace. A growing stench pervaded the lift, threatening to asphyxiate us. I went to remove my mask, but the manager reached out and stopped me. 'The only disadvantage of these skyscrapers,' he said, by way of apology, 'is that we can't open the windows.'

On the top floor, I was assailed by an even more disgusting smell, the stink of the slaughterhouse. In my mind's eye, I had conjured up a terrace with a panoramic view of the town, the countryside and maybe on a clear day, my mountains, even though they were now several days' walk away. Instead, I was confronted with a ballet of carcasses that somersaulted from a water spray to a jet of flame before being quartered with a saw, gutted and propelled into the Paternoster in which they descended back down to the basement, ready to be butchered, processed and packaged for sale.

'Such a lovely drop, isn't it?' exclaimed the director, as he watched the carcasses being flung into the Paternoster. 'But the thing I am most proud of is how we process the blood. It descends the length of the building in these drainpipes where rainwater once flowed. In the time it takes to reach the bottom, it's transformed into black pudding! Ingenious, no? I'll conclude our visit with a single statistic: one hundred and fifty thousand! One hundred and fifty thousand pigs, compared to one thousand five hundred on a similarly sized traditional farm. No more space or land issues, it's all vertical!' he cried in jubilation, gripping my arm. 'I have one last surprise for you.'

He opened a ceiling hatch and ushered me up a ladder. I had finally reached the summit, wearing not an oxygen mask but a sanitary one. What a view! A canopy of skyscrapers every bit as impressive as a virgin forest. The director's voice abruptly broke the spell.

'In that one,' he said, pointing out a transparent skyscraper, 'they grow lettuce, in the one next to it, corn, and in that one, chickens. Did you know, by the way, that they're plucked while they're still alive? An overheated chicken lays less. In those ones, they grow cabbages, raise sheep, cultivate wheat, rapeseed, Jerusalem artichokes, coffee, apricots and tobacco.'

'Whose idea was this?'

'A chap called Fellerheimer. He couldn't breed pigs because of his religion, as unclean animals must not touch the ground. So, he had the idea of raising them above ground level so the earth would not be defiled. We took his idea and used it to solve our escalating space issues. Leeks, pike, oranges, potatoes, mussels...'

'And in that one?' I said, pointing out a skyscraper with no windows.

'Ah,' he said, as we climbed back down the ladder, 'Humans.'

The protracted descent in the Paternoster, with a couple of freshly-quartered carcasses ended with us being joined by a sow about to be inseminated. The heat and stench were unbearable. I was seized by a coughing fit and raised my mask to avoid suffocation. The manager threw me a black look and immediately slapped his gloved hand over my mouth to stop me spreading contamination. Too late. I'd copiously sprayed the sow that was trotting off to join her peers, greeting them with a rub of the snout. Before I left, the manager gave me a chunk of pig's cheese and asked if I would be so good as to send him a photo of our farm once it was up and running. He promised me he would frame and display it in his office as proof that vertical breeding was going global.

It was almost seven o'clock when I emerged onto the street. A pink strip in the sky heralded the imminent onset of night. A delivery man pointed me in the direction of a windowless skyscraper. From behind the sliding screen of a reception desk, a woman whose face was caked in make-up scrutinised me. She had long fingers with painted nails.

'I'd like a room for the night.'

'That'll be twenty-five, paid in advance.'

'Why doesn't the building have windows?'

'To save on curtains.'

I took out my coins, not really expecting her to accept them, but her eyes lit up at the sight of the shining metal. She held out a key and pointed to a staircase.

'Fifth floor. End door. Cage twelve. Be careful, it's a low ceiling. We don't accept liability for accidents.'

'A cage?' I exclaimed.

'A fan is an extra twenty-five,' I heard her shouting through the wall.

The end door wasn't locked. It opened into a narrow corridor, lit intermittently by harsh neon lights and lined with alcoves containing bodies stacked vertically like catacombs, except here the prone figures were alive. Dozens of people sleeping in boxes no bigger than coffins! The corridor branched into two, then into multiple passageways that coiled around the skyscraper like entrails, radiating stifling heat mingled with the reek of supine bodies. A couple of centimetres beneath a neon light was cage twelve: my room. It was a tunnel one metre seventy long by eighty centimetres wide and about half a metre high, equipped with a wooden board by way of a bed. No windows. The only opening, across which was a wire mesh, was onto the corridor. A guy in shorts and sandals cupped his hands so I could climb up to my cage, which was rammed high against the ceiling.

'Do you live here?' I asked, dumbfounded.

'Been here three months. I'm lucky – I was sleeping outside before.'

'I'd rather sleep outside.'

'The police were always hassling us. Didn't want us sticking around messing up the pavements. Bit like chewing gum.'

'Even the pigs have more room!' I cried.

'That's only to be expected. They have to be fattened. Whereas they want us skinny. A skinny deliveryman can weave his way through crowds more easily, guarantees merchandise stays fresh.'

'Where I come from, the dead are laid to rest in this kind of space.'

'They're very fortunate.' I lay down in my tunnel, feet poking out of the end, face grazing the ceiling, with the terrible feeling I was suffocating. I thought about my father, lowered into the ground in a similar position. Was it true that all sons end up like their fathers? I jumped out of the cage and ran headlong down the stairs. 'Fan?' yelled the woman at reception.

Outside, the air hung heavy, but at least you could breathe. I walked through the criss-crossing streets, deserted save for refuse collectors and police officers, both tasked with hunting down the town's garbage, and only stopped when I reached the bridge. At dawn, I would swap places with someone else who had come to fill their shopping bag in this town where there were fields as far as the eye could see. As long as you lay down and looked at the sky.

BARTHOLOMÉ DE MÉNIBUS
30° N 141° W THE LIGHT

The light suddenly flicked on! It was the twentieth of May, twelve days after you left. I was stationed in front of your house, watching for a sign you might be back when I saw a glimmer of light in the living room. Overcome with joy, I limped over to the front door but found it locked. One of the three postage-stamp windows was slightly ajar. Crotchety Christine was in the living room. She was rifling through one of the drawers, holding aloft the storm lantern that she brandished as proof of divine retribution whenever an avalanche cut off our electricity. After much rummaging, she filched a brooch, a few silver spoons and an engraving of your mountain. 'Don't look at me like I'm a thief,' she said, when she spotted me. 'All I'm doing is taking my share of the inheritance.' I retorted that you weren't dead. 'Might as well be,' she spat. Then do you know what she said, that spiteful old spinster? That I'd have liked to help myself to your things too if I'd have been more nimble on my legs! She then vanished down one of the alleyways into the shadows of the overhanging eaves.

The village president made Crotchety Christine return your possessions and threatened to fine anyone who set foot on your property. But, he added, only for forty days after your departure. At the end of this period of grief-in-waiting, your possessions would be shared out among your closest relatives, Crotchety Christine as your first cousin and Jean Tabard on the grounds he was your milk-brother. You know how important milk is to farmers. Forty days! I prayed you would come back before the sixteenth of June, Bartholomé! After that, your key would no longer be proof that you owned your house.

BEHIND THE FIFTH MOUNTAIN

A beat of a drum in the distance. Not of the rain so welcomed by farmers. The sky was cloudless, sheep were snuffling around in the kind of soil that runs through your fingers. I'd been walking for several days across an arid landscape, a marked contrast to my memories of the nearby glacier. On this side of the mountain, the climate changed abruptly, as if the world had been shaken and the pieces stuck back together at random, in a clumsy juxtaposition of hot and cold regions. The drum beats were becoming more audible and I soon caught a glimpse of the rooftops of a town blasted by the scorching wind. Every single wall was crumbling and rotting away. Even the streets seemed to have been created from the erosion of the houses, so narrow, crooked and short-lived were the passageways through them. Back home, snow determined the shape of the village. It shrank or expanded depending on the amount of snow that fell, to the despair of the surveyor's employee who spent his entire time re-measuring it. Here, the town appeared to be shrivelling inexorably. I didn't see a single soul. Had all the people disintegrated too? Only the pulsing of the drum injected a breath of life. But where was the sound coming from? With the wind whirling, it was hard to pinpoint. I eventually spotted a tower that was slightly taller than all the other buildings. There he was, the drummer, producing the sound that carried on the four winds, just like the crier-cum-watchman who announced the time from our church tower and kept a lookout for fires that could destroy the whole village. The drummer was dressed in a long skirt that deployed like a parachute as he spun round and round, quickening the tempo with every turn. Musician, wind, sky and town corkscrewed as he accelerated, wrist pulsating, sky spinning like a top, wind spiralling, town swirling, gyrating, as he gathered more and more speed, skirt parachuting, cheeks plastered flat, the sun undulating, he whirled faster and faster until a final rotation signalled the start of the explosion. A blackish-brown geyser erupted from the earth, propelled to a dizzying height. The dark mass stalled for a second, levitating in mid-air before plummeting back down on the town as thick, nauseating precipitation that splashed the musician's face. He collapsed, utterly drained. Cheering broke out all around the lifeless town, seemingly resuscitated by the fleeting shower. Once the geyser made landfall, heads appeared cautiously from behind deliquescent walls. People gathered in the square and as the women sang, one of the men climbed a step ladder and started speaking.

'My beloved Zambarians, thanks to your excellent timekeeping, we have, once again, saved our town from being bogged down.'

'Hurrah! Hurrah!'

'We must not weaken, for it is a temporary victory. The battle will end when the rain comes. Meanwhile, beloved Zambarians, let us celebrate, let us sing and dance to summon the rain!'

Flutes and string instruments were produced from beneath skirts. Everyone began to dance. The drummer was about to join them when he spotted me. I held out empty hands to show I had come in peace. His gaze settled on my suit, dusty and crumpled from the journey, but whose gold buttons seemed to fascinate him. He offered to swap it for his skirt. I declined politely. Robes were worn by our priest, not our men! Undoubtedly offended by my refusal, he manhandled me towards the village square. The music stopped stone dead. The Zambarians moved aside, clearing a path towards their king. I felt obliged to kneel before him.

'Whose son are you?' he enquired.

'I'm the son of a man called Septime, who has left me orphaned.'

'Where do you come from?'

'The other side of the mountains,' I replied, pointing to the sky.

'Do you bring rain?'

'Rain? Where I'm from, we ask visitors to bring fine weather! I am a simple traveller...'

'Have him clean the town of all this muck, then chop his head off!' he commanded the drummer, who saw the order as a golden opportunity to divest me of my suit.

Astonished murmuring arose from the crowd. I swallowed my saliva, stunned by the king's cruelty. I was led forthwith to the hole gouged out by the geyser. Brown slime splattered the ground.

'It's not oil,' I said, sickened by the stench emanating from it.

'Of course not! It's shit.'

'Do you have a problem with your plumbing?'

'When she blows, that's the problem fixed.'

He handed me a shovel and a brush and pointed at a wheelbarrow and warned me not to get my suit dirty. Water was too precious to be used for cleaning stains, so my job was to scrape up the brown layer and use it to plaster the crumbling walls. I toiled the entire day under a scorching sun. Come evening, they gave me a straw mattress and a greyish porridge that I suspected would block many pipes if ingested. My overseer, the drummer, explained the procedure the king had devised to unblock the sewerage system during the dry season. Once a week, all citizens had to flush their toilets at 9:30 a.m. precisely. The timing was crucial, because only the combined action of each and every citizen could produce enough discharge to unblock the pipes. Under pressure, the amassed excrement was liberated in a single geyser explosion. What could not be predicted was the exact location of the eruption, as it depended on the strength of the pipes and where the excrement had accumulated most. It surfaced somewhere different every week, which explains why the villagers remained holed up in their houses until the stinking rain had ceased.

'It's only a temporary solution until it rains,' sighed the drummer, who was aware the procedure had its limitations. 'When it rains, water pours into the pipes again and makes them as shiny as silver.'

※

The following morning, I continued the hard labour. A villager occasionally stopped and stared pointedly at my mourning suit. My overseer chased them away, for fear they would stake a claim to it. When the heat receded a little, the king paid me a visit. He was accompanied by courtiers fanning him, and preceded by several trumpeters. He inspected my work, marvelled at how clean the village was and, without deigning to look at me, issued his orders.

He may keep his head on his shoulders. He is so efficient that he will clean our discharge every week.'

The drummer looked dejected as he saluted his king. He had lost claim to my suit. I wondered what was worse: losing my head or plastering excrement on walls for the rest of my life.

The day before the weekly unblocking of the pipes, I was granted a rest day. The village was immaculate, the buildings had taken on some semblance of shape again. Unfortunately, the wind picked up at midday, whittling away walls, eroding façades, and flattening the cheeks of any children lingering outdoors. Stretched out on my straw mattress, I thought of my village. On Sundays, we prayed a little and played cards a lot. Sometimes, we could hear the crack of old Roland's rifle in the distance, the echoes magnifying and transforming it into a full-blown military invasion. But we knew we were protected behind our mountains. Protected from ourselves as well, from our hopes and dreams. I eventually fell asleep, overcome by fatigue, convinced my overseer would wake me with his drumming. In the end, it was children who disturbed my slumber. They were touching my skin, which was fairer than theirs.

'Do you wash it with sand?'

'No, water.'

'The ones before you had the same skin.'

'Before me?' I repeated.

'The ones who cleaned the village.'

'There've been others?'

'A boy and a girl, like us.'

'Children?'

'They never told us their names.'

'What happened to them?'

'They ran away. But without water, you don't get far.'

Had they been sent by the king to dissuade me from fleeing? The children scarpered when they saw the drummer on his way, his drum dangling from a shoulder strap. He took me to the tower where he began beating out the alert for all citizens to stand by their toilets. The sun was already high in the sky. The crumbling outlines of the village shimmered in the hot morning air. Not a single Zambarian could be seen in the streets. The drum beats gathered pace, the musician spun round in circles, I began to feel the same giddiness as the previous week. At nine thirty, a final tremor gave the signal. The toilets flushed and emptied in a single swish. Rumbling traversed the bowels of the village. Channelled by pure chance or weaknesses in the pipes, the geyser suddenly spewed into the square, splattering all the houses. Are our brains clogged with useless thoughts too, a kind of spiritual excrement? My grey matter dilated at the exact moment the geyser erupted, and an idea popped into my head. It couldn't have come at a better moment just as a vile brown sludge devoured the square. A mammoth task awaited me!

'I can't bring you rain, but I do know where to find huge quantities of water.'

'Where?' demanded the king.

'Do I have your assurance that, afterwards, I will be freed?'

'I give you my word.'

※

Our convoy departed at dawn the following day. The Zambarians were so suspicious of the tools and equipment I had instructed them to bring that they kept me under close guard the entire journey. It took three days to reach our destination. Every morning, the Zambarians donned an extra robe as protection against the increasingly bitter cold. The king was present. He wanted to be the first to see the water and honour it with a blessing. One day in my village, the priest had blessed the water from a spring he had supposedly discovered. Candles, choirboys, and salt statues had all been wheeled out, as had a small nest egg from the diocese to pay for the celebrations. A week later, the spring had run dry. Still, it was quite a party, the priest had declared with a sly smile. All the talk in the café had been about the leak that Rodolphe of Haut Binet had just repaired in his chalet upstream of the spring. We too had our plumbing story and the priest his miracle. In the afternoon of the third day of walking, I raised my arm.

'It's here!'

The king shoved me aside to be sure he was the first to touch the water, but he suddenly skidded to a halt.

'Where is it? I don't see any water!'

'There, on the ground,' I said, pointing at the frozen lake I had passed on my travels a week or so before.

'This isn't water, it's a mirror!' he exclaimed, signalling to his guards to surround me.

'It's a lake. Go nearer and touch it!'

The king approached cautiously and reached out a hand hesitantly towards the surface.

'This water is hard,' he said, withdrawing it abruptly.

'Look more closely. Do you see something forming on your skin?'

'Ah yes, a few drops of water!'

'It's your body heat making ice crystals melt.'

'So we have to heat this ice, as you call it, to obtain water?'

'Have you not an abundance of sun?'

'But how are we going to transport it? We can't even dip our hands into it!'

'With this!'

As our convoy entered the town, the Zambarians were in the midst of a rain dance. What a waste of time! They crowded round our cargo and were disappointed not to find the much-anticipated basins of water. The king summoned all the citizens to the cramped building where the town's pump station was housed. He ordered the demolition of the roof and walls, which were crumbling away in any case, so that everyone could witness the miracle. The pipework was thus exposed to the open air and the brilliant sun. Copying the techniques I'd shown him, the king produced from under a tarpaulin an ice core a metre long and the exact circumference of the pipes. The crowd murmured in astonishment. With the technical assurance acquired on the return journey, the king explained it was ice and how the water held captive inside it could be released. Then, in the same way one loads a cannon, he inserted the icicle projectile into the pipe. It slid in perfectly with a slight gurgling sound before vanishing into the water mains. His men then inserted all the ice suppositories, harvested by perforating the lake with sections of used pipe to obtain the correct size. Once the cart was empty, the king emitted a small belch of satisfaction as if he were the sewerage system personified, and commanded his people to follow him to the septic tank, which had been empty since the last rainfall.

'In fifteen minutes precisely, the miracle will occur!' he said, with the solemnity I had advised. 'From now on, you shall dance for the sun, not the rain!'

Fifteen minutes later, a tiny brown drip dribbled from the pipe that fed into the rest of the water supply, followed by another, until it became a trickle splashing into the tank. The Zambarians shouted with joy, growing increasingly elated as the water flowed more plentifully. Very quickly, a fetid chockapoo water was gushing from the pipe like the ice-cold water from our village fountain.

For a week, I was feted as a hero, culminating in my being appointed Admiral of the Wastewater. Glorying in the title, I continued on my way, medal firmly pinned to my suit.

BARTHOLOMÉ DE MÉNIBUS
31° N 142° W

I left at dawn on the sixteenth of June, shortly before the vultures invaded your house, Bartholomé. Those villagers who watched me climb the mountain must have thought to themselves that the lame angel wouldn't get far with her limp. As I hadn't come back down the next morning, they probably took a stretcher and went in search of me. Finding neither body nor casualty, the village president would have declared a forty-day period of grief-in-waiting. My house would then have been donated to the church and my possessions shared out among the seasonal workers, as I have no heir. Who would have wanted to marry an incapacitated woman? I didn't care. I left to join you, Bartholomé de Ménibus, the boy with whom I'd shared a school bench and the man I wanted to be sitting next to when twilight came.

On the path up the mountain, I found the tie that you wore to the funeral knotted to a tree. Had you left clues behind so I'd find them? That gave me courage and I carried on walking painfully, leaning on a stick more solid than my leg. I was dragging behind me a sled piled with dozens of books, faithful companions in my solitary life. The runners were losing traction on the pine needles. By evening, I was in the hut, exhausted but with renewed vigour. I didn't light the lantern as you had. I didn't want them to know I'd reached the top. She left, they'd say, and was never seen again. An angel couldn't have done better.

I saw that over the mountain was another mountain, then another and another. Us mountain dwellers are familiar with the echoes that reverberate from one summit to another. The next day, I crossed ravines, clinging to my sled. I careened down slopes faster than if I'd had ten legs, and in a few hours found myself by the side of a road that was very busy, but only in one direction. I decided to walk along the traffic-free side. You love silence and that would have been the side you'd have chosen. I'd only taken a few steps when a strange convoy stopped beside me. It was a boat drawn by four cows, each with a porthole on their rump like the ones on cruise ships. An elderly man, the carriage driver or captain of the vessel for which I had no word, helped me clamber aboard.

The vehicle stopped several times for passengers, who were exclusively the elderly, to board. So I decided to name it the geriatruck. Only people of a certain age were waiting for the geriatruck. After nearly an hour at bovine pace, the driver dropped us off at a barn that was being restored. Two elderly people were heaving themselves up ladders to paint the outside walls, another was replacing rotten planks of wood on the doorstep, a woman was hammering a section of corrugated iron, others were passing up tiles for the roofing. The carriage driver invited us inside. Everyone was working furiously too. Nailing, pulling cables, greasing hinges, making furniture. Those with mobility problems were busy chopping potatoes or sewing curtains. I was told to pick a bed, to make myself at home. I explained to them that I was looking for a man. A young man. They all laughed heartily. No young folk here. What about me? I asked. Why had they let me board the vehicle? Because I limped like they did. And then one of them mentioned the young man in his suit who had restored their dignity by driving them to the barn... Now, instead of dragging their old limbs along the roadside, they were sticking two fingers up at their neglectful families! Although they referred to the young man as their son, was it you, Bartolomé? The son in his mourning suit?

MARIE-JEANNE URECH

BEHIND THE SEVENTH MOUNTAIN

I was crossing a rocky desert, a lunar landscape with little to recommend it. The only landmark a road that apparently led straight to the sea. Was I weeks or months away from my village? I'd left to find out what was behind the mountain, and what had I discovered? Hours of solitude. I'd left on a day of mourning and what had I found out? That my family was that village, a village so small that it would have fitted into my pocket, had I left on good terms, embracing each person in turn. But the thirst for adventure was pushing me farther away, in the direction of the sea, a fitting end to the journey of a fresh Admiral of the Wastewater. A queue of trucks had formed at a crossroads and was filtering slowly to the left. A musician was playing a barrel organ by the wayside. The drivers were throwing coins in his direction and a monkey dressed in red scampered to pick them up. The musician raised his cap and ushered them through. When it was my turn, I threw a coin at him too. If he decided to go to my village one day, he could at least afford to treat himself to a glass of schnapps. The monkey caught the coin in mid-air, then jumped on me and played with my admiral's medal, which shone more brightly than the coins.

'Séraphin,' his master ordered, 'leave the man alone and give him his coin back.'

'Keep it, it's my pleasure.'

'I'm not asking for charity, sir. The drivers are paying a toll.'

'Well, please keep it. I would like to take this road too.'

'You can't.'

'Why not? Where does it go?'

'To a cemetery.'

'I lost my father a short while ago.'

'My condolences, sir. Unfortunately for you, only trucks are allowed.'

※

'So, what...?'

'Please don't insist, sir.'

The monkey bared his teeth at me, the musician turned the crank and I pretended to be on my way, but hid behind a rock instead. I was intrigued by this cemetery. I must have listened to the barrel organ's entire repertoire at least three times before I realised what was going on – the procession of trucks and the accompanying turns of the crank were a kind of perpetual movement. The musician wouldn't leave his post until nightfall, if indeed he left at all. As children during the haymaking season, we used to hop aboard the village president's trailer as he was the only one who owned a mechanical tractor. We'd secretly hitch a ride up the hill, and when we got to the village, we'd jump out of the vehicle covered in hay, startling the villagers like scarecrows did birds. With these memories in mind, I snuck under the trailer of one of the trucks near the front axle. We drove for a good ten minutes on a surprisingly smooth road before slowing down. I jumped off behind a rocky outcrop. What I then witnessed was something no villager should ever have to see: they who honour their dead on a precarious patch of earth adjoining a church; they who raise their caps whenever they pass a war memorial engraved with twelve names at most, though that would often be a third of the men. Stretched out before me was a cemetery full of crosses forming diagonal lines as far as the eye could see. Dozens of gaping holes awaited their corpses while, receding into the distance, gravediggers dug new ones. The trucks drove between the rows, depositing their lugubrious loads next to each grave. A man, probably a priest – from that distance, shapes were all I could make out – uttered a few quick words, after which the deceased were interred under shovel-loads of earth. What war was decimating so many people? What epidemic? What cataclysm? Nothing had been reported in our newspaper; news doesn't cross these mountains.

I emerged from my hiding place and walked towards a grave, curious to find an explanation for the carnage. The crosses were hastily manufactured affairs and provided no answers. A series of numbers that were neither dates of birth nor death provided the only identification.

'Hey you! You shouldn't be here!' A man yelled, catching me unawares. I was about to turn and run when he added: 'Follow me, we need you at deliveries.'

A few diagonals further on, a row of empty holes awaited us. A truck had just arrived and the driver, helped by two men who I'd taken for gravediggers from a distance, were tugging off the tarpaulin.

'Here's the list,' the man said to me, holding out a document. 'We're ready to bury them.'

I stood there, concentrating on the document that contained a series of numbers, also in rows. Fortunately, the driver, who was clearly working to a tight schedule, didn't notice my confusion and started unloading the truck. The two gravediggers were leaning on their spades, staring at me, evidently waiting for me to say something before starting the burial. Thinking they might have taken me for a clergyman because of my suit, I went up to the graveside and crossed myself, clumsily mimicking our priest.

※

'What's that all about?' one of the gravediggers whispered to the other.

'Dunno, but it's not numbers.'

'We commit this body to the ground,' I continued, in an uncertain voice.

'What's he rabbiting on about?'

'The reference number will do,' the other man interjected. 'We've got thirty more of these to dump...'

'Dump!' I shouted indignantly. 'Is that how you do burials here?'

'Burials? Barrels. We say barrels here.'

'The pronunciation's not important! Just give me enough time to say a prayer for them,' I said, forgetting that I was neither priest nor welcome here.

'A prayer, what on earth for?'

'For the salvation of their souls.'

The driver honked his horn, concerned about his schedule.

❇

'Just say the reference number, so we can fill in the hole...' implored the first man.

'This man will have his prayer!' I declared, standing firm. 'After what must have happened to him, I dare say he'll need it.'

'What? Look down and tell me if you see a man...'

As he was being so insistent, I glanced down and, in the ground, I saw a metal barrel.

'Odd shape, your coffins.'

'They're not coffins, they're barrels. What is wrong with you?'

'You bury your dead in a sitting position?'

'Where did they find this one? There is no man inside...'

'So what's worth burying if it's not a man?' I shot back.

'Nuclear waste, dammit!'

❇

The shock almost blew me off my feet. The kind of fields I knew were full of wheat, but here I was standing on a minefield. Invisible mines that caused invisible, sinister and irreversible damage. I was about to run, to escape as fast as I could from this cemetery where they buried living matter, when the driver yelled from his truck: 'Get on with it! We can't leave that lot out in the open.'

Cutting short my funeral address, I recited the series of numbers as required and was then told to write them on the cross. This identified each barrel so that, if it leaked, the finger of blame could be pointed at nuclear power station X or Y, which would then issue an apology for the inconvenience caused. Once the barrel was buried and the cross planted in the earth, we moved on to the neighbouring plot and carried on for a row of thirty. I did so well that my initial hesitation was soon forgotten, and they slapped me on the back, encouraging me to return the following day. I shook my head.

'If you're concerned about your blood cells, we're paid ten times more than anywhere else.'

'You die quicker too,' I said gloomily.

'With ten times more money, you can live ten times faster. We make up for it where we can.'

In the village, we've never seen a nuclear power station. It's a spectre of the flatlands. But we did fight the windmills and win. A white-collar type from the capital wanted to build eight turbines on the ridge. We spoke as one, and the village president communicated our refusal. There was no way we wanted our landscape desecrated to produce energy that we didn't need. Nonetheless, one fine day some engineers alighted from the red train. My father guided them up to the ridge and, taking advantage of the bad weather, 'lost' them on the other side of the mountain. We never saw them again. Not one to mess with, the patriarch! When the blades arrived a few weeks later, we chopped them up for firewood. In the capital, they were convinced that eight turbines were turning at full tilt, providing energy for the entire valley. They weren't entirely wrong because the wood provided our heating for that whole winter. I was still smiling at the memory of how we'd tricked them when I found myself face-to-face with the barrel organ, the monkey and its master. I'd walked right back to the entrance without realising. The melody stopped abruptly.

'So, you entered without my permission?' said the musician angrily.

'I found a job.'

'Undertaker?' he asked, looking at me and my suit scornfully.

'Inspector. It's my writing on the crosses.'

'Good for you! So now you owe me something.'

'What?'

'The coin to get in.'

'I gave you one.'

'Séraphin gave it back.'

'No, he didn't. He kept it.'

'Poor little Séraphin, he's implying you're a thief.' The monkey cocked his head, eyebrows scrunched, and started crying into his master's lap, chest heaving with huge sobs. 'There, there, Séraphin. He isn't as bad as all that, and I'm sure he'll give you his captain's medal. That'll put the smile back on your face.'

'It's admiral... Admiral of the Wastewater.' I corrected, proud of my gloriously acquired title.

The monkey pinched the medal and began hopping up and down.

'Are you leaving the cemetery?'

'I hope so, yes.'

'Well, that'll be one coin. One to get in, one to get out.'

'Daylight robbery,' I grumbled, digging in my pockets.

I searched in the folds of my suit lining, but all I managed to unearth was a velvet pouch. I untied it as the musician looked on greedily, having given up turning his crank, too busy dreaming of the fortune I was about to reveal. As luck would have it, I couldn't find a single coin.

'I reckon you'll have to spend the night in the cemetery,' he said as he started grinding out a melody, initially discordant then perfectly in tune.

I could have carried on my way without his permission as I'd done before, but an idea was taking root in my mind, propelling me back towards the cemetery despite the danger.

Normally, seeds are scattered from a hessian sack tied around the waist, not a velvet pouch more suited to jewels. Normally, we would consult the moon, the almanac or old Roland. Normally, we would choose a well-ploughed field. But that was on the other side of the mountain. If you'd have been on this side, you'd have seen a man in his Sunday best sowing seeds between the crosses on the loose soil of the freshly dug graves, above thousands of radioactive barrels, sowing seeds, as I was saying, in the hope that the cemetery would become a field of wheat, rye and barley.

Who had slipped the seeds into my suit pocket? Had they already been there at the funeral? Should I have scattered them on my father's grave like you throw a rose on a coffin? Was it you, little lame angel?

BARTHOLOMÉ DE MÉNIBUS
31° N 141° W

+SVIZRA is a series of eight chapbooks showcasing contemporary writing translated from the four official languages of Switzerland: German, French, Italian and Romansh. In giving equal visibility to each of the four languages, **+SVIZRA** offers a range of Swiss writing never before seen in English from a diverse group of some of the best authors living and working in Switzerland today, including National Literature Prize winning Anna Ruchat, Iraqi exile Usama Al-Shahmani and treasured Romansh author, Rut Plouda.

+SVIZRA is the result of Strangers Press' latest exciting collaboration with an international group of authors, translators, publishers, designers and editors, all made possible by generous funding from Pro Helvetia.

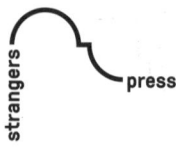

Supported By

University of East Anglia

NORWICH
UNIVERSITY
OF THE ARTS